Clint Faraday Mysteries
Book Final
Death Closes the Case

Clint is old and can't move around like he used to. He feels useless because he can't work with his people much.

He still can solve mysteries!

This one involves a lot of people. Innocent bystanders. It is a scheme being run by very powerful people.

Can the famous Clint Faraday find a way to end this threat to his people?

Contents

About the author

CD Moulton has traveled extensively over much of the world both in the music business, where he was a rock guitarist, songwriter and arranger and in an import/export business. He has been everything from a bar owner to auto salvage (junkyard) manager, longshoreman to high steel worker, orchid grower to landscaper, tropical fish farmer to commercial fisherman. He started writing books in 1983 and has published more than 250 books as of January 1, 2015. His most popular books to date are about research with orchids, though much of his science fiction and fantasy work has proven popular. He wrote the CD Grimes, PI series and the Det. Nick Storie series, Clint Faraday series and many other works.

He now resides in Puerto Armuelles, Panamá, where he writes books, plays music with friends, does research with orchids and medicinal plants – and pursues his favorite ways to spend his time: beach bum and roaming the mountain jungles doing his botanical research. He has lately become involved in fighting for the rights of the indigenous people, who are among his closest friends, and in fighting the extreme corruption in the courts and police in Panamá.

He offers the free e-book, *Fading Paradise*, that explains what he has been through because of the corruption.

CD is involved in research of natural cancer cure at this time. It has proven effective in all cases, so far. It is based on a plant that has been in use for thousands of years, is safe, available, and cheap. He has studied botany, and was cured of a serious lymphoma with use of the plant, *Ambrosia peruviana*.

Information about this cure is free on the FaceBook page, Ambrosia peruviana for cancer. CD asks only that all who try it please report on its effectiveness on that group.

Death Closes the Case

A Threat

Clint Faraday, retired PI from Florida, USA, now living on the comarca Ngobe Bugle in Panamá, rubbed his swollen knee and grunted. It was getting to the point where he couldn't function well when any physical action was required.

He had been exceptionally lucky for most of his life. He was always healthy and able. Now, at 89 years, it was catching up with him. He had to accept the simple fact that he couldn't run around like a twenty year old anymore. When he hurt himself, he stayed hurt. He didn't heal at a tenth the rate he used to.

He was fortunate that he still had his mental facilities. He could still solve a puzzle.

He had become expert on finding information on the internet. He just recently had run down a scheme by a bunch of sleazy politicians to take some of the comarca land where they would build casinos and hotels on the pristine beaches on the Caribbean. They had bribed some top people in the government to declare the land was national land that was open for ROP settlement that could be filed upon and title purchased after two years. The files were backdated to allow the scum to start building as soon as the title was cleared, which would have taken 45 days.

It was comarca land. The whole thing was a scam to steal the land. An old story. Clint knew how that one worked, so was able to have three big names jailed for two years on corruption charges and have two big mobsters deported. The comarca land was re-certified.

It was hushed up to a great extent by the corruption in the courts and police. That was part of the scheme.

He didn't have to leave his house on the island just out from Cusapín for that. The reason he was still alive was because he was living on the comarca, was declared Ngobe, the second person to ever be accorded that honor, and the comarca wouldn't allow anyone to go to where he was. The Indigenos take care of their own.

Tyna, his younger wife, still a beautiful woman at 67 years of age, came with a glass of guanabana chicha.

"Nito (their son, now head of police on the comarca) called and said to tell you to stop acting like a teenager," she said. "I told him I've tried to get that through to you for thirty or forty years."

She laughed, along with him.

He sighed and asked if Nicole had called yet. She was heading the hospital on this end of the comarca.

"She said she has you scheduled to meet with Dr. Schrader, in Bocas Town, day after tomorrow. Dr. Salardes studied under him. He's a specialist about aging."

"Huh! I age. I'm almost ninety, so I have to slow down. I've been slowing down 'til I'm sick of it! I can't even go to the garden to dig yuca anymore! I'm becoming a useless drag on you and the people!"

"Don't be ridiculous! You just saved more than five hundred hectares of comarca land from being stolen! That's hardly a drag on the people! It's as far from useless as you can get!

"As for me, I can't picture life without you. You're my happiness and my reason for going on. You and the kids.

"Nicole is pregnant. Mathilde says it will be a healthy boy

she will name Carlos Faraday Jimenez."

"And Nito named his kids Tyna and Guillermo Faraday Vega. The Faradays are going to be like Smith in a few generations, I think.

"Why Guillermo?"

"Because Guillermo is still a prize gigolo stud at fifty eight years of age. You know how Nito is about sex."

"Yeah. Do I have to go to Bocas?"

"You promised."

"Shit!"

It was known far and wide that any promise made by Clint Faraday would be kept. Period. Pass me a beer.

"When do I have to be there?"

"Day after tomorrow at ten o'clock. We can go to Bocas tomorrow afternoon. Judi says our house there is vacant right now, so we can go directly there."

"If I have to, I have to. Shit!"

Clint tied to his dock at Bocas Town on Isla Colón and waved to Judi Lum, the attractive Oriental woman who had helped him with his cases when he first came to Panamá. She was in her early seventies and was still a striking woman. She still ran the hospital and clinic construction on the comarcas. Clint had made millions of dollars as a detective, mostly by accident. She came over as Tyna was unpacking their clothes for the next few days.

"Hi, Jude! Anything new and different happen here?" Clint greeted.

"Same old same old. Same old crooks with new faces – along with most of the old faces. The sixth street crowd has moved over past the airport, which is good. The police can watch them a lot easier. You know that Jim died last year.

Tom came whining back from Ecuador and proceeded to get his ass kicked twice in one week. He decided to go back to Vermont or wherever."

Tom was a pain in the ass type who knew everything there was to know about anything. His only trouble was the parts he got wrong, such as the facts. He gossiped about people and got into trouble with it. He refused to learn.

"Couldn't happen to a more deserving person," Clint replied. "What happened with Manny?"

"Manny Matthews" was actually Marko Bocinni, a major crime syndicate head from California who Clint had established on Isla San Cristóbal. He had been a lot of help in Clint's cases because of his power and connections in the underworld. He had worked with Clint and Judi with the hospitals and clinics, and was a respected pillar of the community. He had made the mob go legitimate. It was his father who has been the big mafia don.

"He developed a serious lung problem and moved to somewhere in the Mediterranean – like we told people he did thirty five years ago. He can't take the humidity here in a rain forest. His kids are taking over the stuff here. They're a lot like he is. It's good to know things will stay the same with our projects.

"There is one problem that nobody knows about, though. I heard some things and had Tony check them out through his dad. Something's afoot here that could be bad news for everyone."

Judi was the best information gatherer Clint ever knew. She could drop a word or phrase into a conversation, get an answer, act like she didn't hear it – and was talking about something else, anyway, and find things in an hour it would take Clint and detective methods a month to find.

"What sort of thing? I'm not doing the detective bit anymore. I can't get around well enough to be playing that part."

"It affects the comarca in some way I haven't learned yet. Politics."

"We just solved that one. They're gone!"

"No. Maybe some of the same people, but something different, something the CIA might be behind. I think it has to do with that big copper lode and some other minerals they found with the satellites."

"Well, I'll try to stay out of it. I might do some tracing with the comps and such. Maybe I'll find something."

"Yeah. CD and Alma and Nick and Janet take lessons from Clint in that part of it," Tyna said. "Clint has to be careful. There are some scary people around lately."

"These are mostly Panamanian. You know how the CIA works," Judi warned.

"Brother! Do I!"

They chatted for awhile. Judi and Tyna went to town to get a few groceries. Clint turned on his computer and checked out what he could find, then went into town to see who was still around. He didn't know many of the present bunch.

He was going past Refugios as two men were going in. One was a man Clint caused to be thrown out of Panamá ten years ago as an undesirable. He was involved with a plot to steal an Indio's land out past Puerto Armuelles. The other was a judge from Chiriqui. A judge who was under suspicion of corruption a few years ago.

Suddenly Judi's hints looked like they could stand a wee bit better investigation.

Milton Forbes turned just then and spotted Clint. He said something to Judge Raul Rancheros, who turned to stare.

Clint had exceptional peripheral vision. He didn't appear to look at them. Rancheros shook his head, then looked confused, then shrugged.

So. They weren't certain it was him. That could be a plus.

Clint kept walking. They went on inside the restaurant.

This was getting interesting. Clint wasn't in a position where he could learn anything, at the moment, but he was damned well going to learn some things.

He went on back to his house. Tyna and Judi were cooking up one of the recipes they learned about years ago. He said Forbes and Rancheros were in town. He wanted to know what they were up to. No matter what, it was to no good. Not those two! The women agreed.

He fired up the computer and sat back to think. He had to have a reference point to start an investigation.

Okay. Judi said copper and such. That had been going on for about fifty years. The government kept trying to take the Indigeno land. They would open-pit mine and leave a huge scar on the Earth that would last centuries. The Indios wouldn't permit it.

Milton Forbes was into that uranium scam, where they were trying to smuggle out enough to build a dirty nuclear bomb.

There was no uranium in the area where they were trying to get in. Forbes probably had the connections to handle other vital metals.

Rancheros was just a corrupt judge. He would have the setup that would allow stealing land, but the comarca wasn't a smart place to try it. He would try to nationalize the land – which wouldn't have much chance, either.

But Judi said the CIA was involved. That could mean a very big problem for everyone. Their record for doing anything positive was non-existent, almost.

Find out who else is involved. All he could do now was hypothesize. That was a fast track to nowhere.

How corny!

He called Tony, Marko's son. Tony said he would get the organization to check things out.

Clint sat back to think. It was a matter of waiting until he had more information. If there was a company or engineer involved it would give him a place to start.

Forbes and Rancheros had seen him. They would check to find he was there.

Clint went to a box of computer parts and accessories to take out several spycams and audio pickups. He had places to put them where not an inch of the inside of the house would be missed. He took out a backup computer and put it into the little space he designed to hide it. He hooked up everything and tested it.

He was called to dinner. It was delicious.

Judi and Tyna would go into town to visit friends. Clint said he didn't feel like walking that much, so he'd stay around there and work with the computer.

He didn't want to scare them, so didn't tell them about the precautions he was taking. He did make a note about the whole system and where the comp was that ran the surveillance and so forth. He put it in the files under household expenses in the folder for gas and electric. Judi knew about that because they'd used the method to trade information when they felt the house was bugged or worse. Even when he went back to Cusapín he could let her know to check it regularly. The system worked on sound and motion activation as well as breaker beams and such.

He then took a cold Balboa Ice out to the deck to sit

watching the bay at sunset.

This was a peaceful place. The town, two minutes walk away, was a typical Caribbean tourist trap, but here, this close, it was quiet and tranquil.

He wanted it to stay that way.

The phone rang, so he groaned out of the chair and answered it.

"Mr. Faraday? I wish to know what you are doing here. You will tell me, because I am sitting in the park not fifty feet from your wife and neighbor."

Clint had to bite his tongue to stop himself from saying what he thought at that moment.

"I have a doctor's appointment in the morning. It isn't any of your business. If you threaten me or my wife or my friends or my people, you have gone too far. There's no going back.

"Who are you and what do you care where I am or what I'm doing?"

The caller hung up. Clint had to control his temper. He was sure that was Forbes. The gringo accent and phraseology told him that.

Wasn't it? It was a gringo with an education. If it wasn't Forbes it was someone in his group.

Why didn't he speak in English? Rancheros and Forbes certainly knew it was his native language. Both spoke English.

It wasn't Forbes. Forbes' Spanish wasn't quite that good. It wasn't Rancheros. Rancheros' was a lot better.

Whatever and whoever, they had threatened Clinton Faraday's wife and a friend. They started out by going too far.

They were going regret doing that. Bitterly!

The doctors probed and twisted and yanked at him, then came to the decision that he was getting older and had to adjust his life to that fact. He was in better shape than most people who were in their sixties and had taken care of themselves.

He wouldn't heal as fast. He was lucky in that he always ate natural foods, so calcium wasn't taken out of his system. His skeletal structure was exceptionally good. His eyes and ears were very good, far better than most in their sixties. He was still able in the sexual parts, though his prostate was slightly enlarged. No hint of cancer there. No signs of Alzheimers. No liver deterioration. Unclogged arteries. A small shadow on the MRI, but it probably wasn't too serious, though it was in an inoperable spot in his brain. They would have to watch it. He would come back in one week for a follow-up.

So he would owe them a couple of hundred bucks to tell him what he already knew. It would make Tyna feel better, so it was worth it, for that. She was his most basic care, nowadays. If there was one worry he didn't have, it was money. He still had over eight million dollars in the bank, though he had given the comarca and friends a lot of millions, particularly in building schools and hospitals and such.

He got back to the house at ten to six. Tyna left a note to go to Ben's place for dinner, so he checked the comp surveillance. Nothing.

He walked to Ben's for the gourmet meal.

Ben Longstreet was a gay man who had been a friend

since Clint moved to Panamá. Earl, his lover, came a bit later. They had been a couple since.

Dinner was large shrimp stuffed with a crabmeat and vegetable filling, breaded, and deep fried in olive oil with a bit of garlic, a salad made of lettuce, pineapple, maraschino cherries, and white grapes with a light dressing Earl whipped up. Steamed broccoli and cauliflower in a cheese sauce, and good old French fried potatoes. Dessert was guanabana ice cream, homemade.

They discussed only pleasant things during the meal. After, Clint managed to bring up the fact Forbes and Rancheros were in town. Ben had seen them, but just walking on the street. They were with some lawyer from David or somewhere.

Clint and Tyna went back to the house for the night. Judi and Ben and Earl went into town.

Tyna and Clint puttered around, fixing things that needed fixing. They went to bed a little after midnight, and were up with the dawn, as usual. Tyna said she was anxious to get back to the island. A day was plenty of Bocas Town for her! It wasn't so bad, now that so much had moved to Boca del Drago, but she liked home. BT would never be home.

"Judi will go with us. She likes the island and wants to see Alma and Janet," Tyna said. "She can be ready anytime we say. I told her it would be early."

Clint grunted, then went to the comp. He had a couple of answers from Tony. The lawyer with Rancheros, Forbes, Robinson and Flores was someone named Penceros, from near Frontera.

Penceros? That sounded familiar.

He checked his names list on the comp. Penceros was tied up in that corruption case in Frontera. He was a sleazeball with a lot of excuses for everything he did. It was always somebody else's fault.

They were looking for more financing. What it was wasn't clear, but Tony could get an operative from the old mob to act interested in investing in something that would turn enough fast profit for a few unreported funds to be added without anyone noticing. They were all crooks, so would respond to another crook.

It had to do with land, but not the land itself. It wasn't stated anywhere in a way that would tell them anything.

"Ty, I'm staying here for a few days. You and Judi can go. I have to check out some things. I think there's going to be a lot of trouble for the comarca if we don't put an end to it. I want to know what those crooks are up to."

Tyna knew it would be pointless to even try to change his mind. She warned him that he didn't have the police here on his side nearly so much as in the past.

"I think, with the ones here, the police would be a bad place to depend on. Those are the type who own some higher-ups in the courts and police."

"Well, be careful. You can't go running around like you used to."

"That's what the doctors said. I have to slow down. I think I can find out a few things and have Tony handle anything that needs handling."

She nodded, sighed, and said she'd take the boat over to pick up Judi. Keep in touch. If it gets dangerous, come home. Let Tony handle it.

He nodded. He helped her and Judi pack the boat and kissed her goodbye when they left.

As soon as they were gone he grabbed the phone and made a call to a woman he knew, a woman who was now head of the news department on a very popular TV network.

"Juliene? Clint Faraday here. Care to help light a fire under a few really big slimewad crooks? It could get damned dangerous. Possible CIA involvement."

"Clint? I haven't heard from you in ten years! I'm in!"

"We have to have a way open to be able to get a lot of publicity fast. That means moving before they get a foothold. Here's the basics and what I think might work.

"First, we collect a lot of...."

Clint went to sit in the Golden Grill. He had been going there for more than thirty years. There was a group who were always there for breakfast and coffee and chat. He had stayed around the comarca and went to David a few times the past five years. He had quit the detective bit to a great extent, except when the comarca, his people, needed him.

Penceros was sitting at a table in front and almost fell off the chair when Clint came to say "Buenos dias!" Clint had saved him from a big jail sentence with the promise he would straighten up his act. If he went back to his old ways, he would pay a high price.

"Faraday?! I thought you'd be dead by now! I wouldn't ... I mean, it's good to see you're still active!"

"Not very anymore. It creeps up on you. I stay around the comarca most of the time. It's a lot more tranquil than here or David, and I don't spend so much time in Tula. I can't take a six kilometer hike up the mountains every time I need food or such. Give me the flat ground.

"How are things with you? Keeping busy?"

"Er, um, yes, more or less. I'm checking out investment properties and that kind of thing."

"Too late here. It's done. Maybe around Chiriqui Grande,

but that's not the best place anymore. More in Chiriqui. Frontera to Puerto Armuelles is growing fast. There's still some property there that could be a good investment. Most of Tierra Oscura is national land that they can't hope to work around for that kind of development."

"It's beginning to shift away from the coast and into the mountains, but a lot of that is in the permanent preserves. They're finding some ... things.

"I have to meet an appointment. Good to see you!"

He got up and left. Clint smirked. He wondered if Penceros knew just how bad a slip he'd made there. They'd found something. The scam artists had something they could turn into a lot of money ... or ... they could make a lot of money claiming they found something.

He would have to find which. He called Tony to ask him to listen around, then called Juliene to say she should check the files to see what was reported that wasn't reported about a few areas.

"Reported but not reported? Like pressure to bury it or that didn't have enough backup?"

"Yeah."

"Ahh! Both."

"Uh-huh. I'm trying to find a reason."

"Inland and in the mountains. Fortuna or the comarca?"

"I think anything in La Fortuna is already found, if it's that big a thing."

They chatted awhile, catching up on things. Clint soon was sitting drinking coffee and thinking. He knew where there were several things they could be interested in, but they were in the center of the comarca, more or less. Amethyst (Book 50: *Where Death Waits*) and gold (Book 33: *Die Trying*) were the most likely that he knew about.

It was going to be a matter of tying one of them – or more – to those things they could use as a basis for a scam. They might also think they could actually mine them.

Not likely. The gold was in a place that was as inaccessible as you could want. The amethyst was, too, when you considered it.

But you could take pictures of it ... the gold. It had to be that, because no one could hope to live to take pictures of the amethyst.

There could be other things. If the people in the comarca knew about them they wouldn't mention them. They have little or no importance to comarca life.

It wouldn't be the phosphate (Book 19: *A Moving Target*) because that was in relatively flat land near the Caribbean. It wouldn't be uranium (Book 11: *See You in Hell*). That was in Chiriqui Province, near Puerto Armuelles, There was some silver there, too. It was a lot closer to Volcan Barú.

Silver could be in the other mountain areas. There was zinc and lead and some cinnabar. Very secondary considerations. Topaz and jade were tertiary considerations.

Oil was a scam, but everyone knew that.

Clint went over everything in his mind, the locations and conditions in which it was found.

It had to be silver, but what was known wasn't from the comarcas.

But it was known. Not new finds.

Crap! There was a lot of silver that was made into trinkets – a long way from where the known mines were. Not far into the comarca. East of La Fortuna and west of the peninsula where he was staying where Cusapín was the tip. It could be arranged to enter from national land at Fortuna, which was actually comarca land. It was mountainous and several things were there, mostly smaller lodes.

Was the CIA bit a diversion? Was it not involved at all?

Clint remembered several cases where he came across the CIA. That voodoo queen who thought she could take over the economy of Central America or something as nutcase. (book 7: *Comedy of Terrors*) The latest he remembered was with that derelict ship (Book 48: *Dead in the Water*). There could be a CIA agent who was looking for personal gain.

He didn't have any other ideas. He was just finishing his coffee when Forbes came in and directly to him.

"What are you doing here, Faraday?"

"Minding my own business. I have a house here, as you very well know. I might ask what you're doing here, seeing you were declared persona non grata by Panamá.

"You, Penceros, Rancheros ... maybe I should look into a thing or two. I was out of the business, but you three ... maybe I will look into a thing or two! I wouldn't have considered it until you came on with this bullshit. I would have gone back to the comarca the day after tomorrow and not thought of it until whatever you're up to hits the news."

"You get involved in this, you won't live to watch the news, old man!"

Clint surprised himself with the speed with which he stood and delivered a good solid right to the jaw of Forbes, who went down on the sidewalk and into the gutter.

"You threatened me and have my answer, dickhead! Don't make the mistake of getting in my face again! Your demise will be the thing on the news!"

A local cop ran up with a drawn sidearm he pointed at Clint. Clint said he would show him the papers that would explain some things and took the folder he carried when he might need it from his back pocket. He got out the paper, which was a commendation and authorization for him to act as a ranking police officer anywhere in Panamá.

"He threatened me. I responded. I'll let it be a resolved personal dispute – unless he wants to take it further."

"You assaulted me right here in public! I damned well will take it further!" Forbes almost screamed. "It's a lie! I never threatened anyone! He's a liar!"

Clint took the mini-recorder from his shirt pocket. "Care to have a charge of making a false statement to an investigating police officer by a person ejected from this country as undesirable?"

Forbes stared at the recorder.

"In addition; I'm over seventy five. You'd better check the laws here about assaulting anyone my age. You get three years automatically for that – if I make a complaint.

"I don't make one, you don't make one. Ball's in your court."

Forbes turned and stalked off. "He was declared undesirable and ejected?" The officer asked.

"Uh-huh. Don't worry about it unless he pulls another stupid stunt."

"You're Clint Faraday? My professor at the academy talks about you all the time. He says you taught him most of what he knows. Sergio Valdez."

"We worked a lot of cases together. I think I broke something in my hand when I smacked that asshole idiot."

They talked a minute, then Clint headed for his house. *Apparently, that bunch thinks I know a lot more than I do. I'll have to remedy that.*

His hand really did hurt like hell. He went into the house and wrapped it with a tight Ace Bandage.

There was no action on the spycams. Clint worked for

awhile with the comp, then headed for Refugios for a few beers and some talk with the people there. It wasn't the same without Dave and his friends playing music. They had music, but more Latin flavored. Salsa, which Clint didn't care much for.

He went from there to Toro Loco. It wasn't the same, either. The better places were relocating to Drago.

Paulo Robinson and Enrique Flores came in. They avoided Clint, but stared at him a lot. He ignored them, so far as directly looking at them went. He kept them in sight with his peripheral vision.

Penceros and Rancheros came in. They talked animatedly with Flores and Robinson a bit, then Penceros came to ask if he could have a word.

"Have several. They're small. Have a seat."

He sat. "Mr. Faraday, you have caused some trouble for myself and some friends. I will admit you also helped me when I most needed it.

"We are trying to start a business project here. We don't wish to have competition move in before we're ready to compete, in a manner of speaking. Is that why you're here? To learn what we plan so someone else can grab the idea from us?

"It's a matter of the financing, basically. If there are any problems at this point our financing could fall through.

"I know you don't lie. You will either answer me honestly or will not answer. Is that why you are here?"

"No. I came here to a doctor's appointment. I was called on the phone by Flores – I remember his voice – and threatened. I was then assaulted with threats by Forbes.

"Until that time, I didn't much give a damn what you were up to.

"The ass threatened me, for which I don't give a shit. He threatened my wife and my friend. For that, I give a hell of a lot more than a shit. Now I'm going to see what you're up to. If it's all that innocent you wouldn't be pulling this crap."

"Mr. Faraday, Flores called you because of what you caused him in the past, not because of anything the rest of us suggested."

"I didn't cause him anything in the past. He caused it."

"We look at it differently."

"Yes. You feel that the person who catches you at some slimy crooked deal causes what happens to you as a result. It never occurs to you that getting into the slime was your doing, and what happens as a result is your doing."

Penceros sat there in silence a moment.

Clint shook his head. "If you were legitimate you'd simply tell me what you're doing and I'd either agree that it's legitimate or say that it isn't. You make it look like you're up to something crooked that you don't dare tell me about."

"We want to mine an ore that no one here knows about. We're trying to get permits and such set up that will guarantee we don't lose our asses in it."

Clint decided to take a chance. "You aren't getting any permits to mine silver or anything else on the comarca."

He almost fell out of the chair. "HOW DID..!? I mean, what makes you think we're wanting anything on the comarca. I assure you, what we're after won't be on the comarca. That I can say definitely."

"But it is now. I'm not stupid."

"We'll buy the land! That's no problem!"

"You can't buy anything on the comarca. Land isn't for sale there."

"Enough money, they'll change the law."

"Except you don't have half enough money to bribe anyone on the comarca. The museum (Book 51: *Dead Man Talking*) brings in more than a million dollars every three days. It's down a bit now, but it had more than ten years where it did that. The funds in the bank are drawing eight hundred thirty thousand dollars a day. The mines above Quebrada Tula, that aren't operating, could yield several billion dollars and can be carried out with horses where it won't screw up the Earth for a couple of square kilometers. That means you will bribe government officials and legislators and judges. I think you've overestimated the amount of ore there. You won't get your money back."

"Plus you gave them millions. We won't try to bribe anyone on the comarca. You've proven that won't work."

"No we built several millions dollars worth of schools and hospitals. That's a much different thing. It's to help my people. That's what being Ngobe's about.

"Now you can stop the bullshit and tell me what you're so worried about if everything's so hunky-dory."

Penceros stared again. "You can have some of the partners expelled from Panamá. We can't finish without them. We can't allow that."

"Interesting to see how you stop me if you give me reason."

"They don't care how they do it. You did me a big favor. I don't want any of this. I didn't think you'd ever know anything about it."

"Get away from them."

"You've said, many times, that there are things you get into and can never get out of. It's happened with me. You can't have a place for me this time. I'm in and am going to get out when I'm dead. There's no other way.

"I've suggested that they simply wait. You have to be nearing eighty years old, though you don't look it."

"I'm eighty nine."

"So. I'm sure they'll wait. It wasn't something that has to be done today. We'll simply refrain from doing anything that will cause notice. You have nothing but to have a couple of us expelled. We can be back in very little time. Judge Rancheros is the only one of the partners who is over forty. He's forty three

"Have a pleasant evening, Mr. Faraday." He got up and went to his partners. Clint sat, looking thoughtful.

Could he do something to thwart them? They could do nothing and wait for him to kick off and probably could engineer some crooked way to steal everything from his people. That was *not* going to happen.

He was going to get a lot of stuff together that would stop their little plan. He would leave it with Judi and Ben, who would get a lot of publicity with it at the worst possible time.

They had to be unaware he was doing that. They could counter if they knew what he planned.

Clint looked over the papers he'd put in three stacks. It was, first, a record of the times he'd come across those people, the results, and an added form asking why they were there, the ones who were declared persona non grata in Panamá. He scanned the whole package to memory stick and made three copies of it.

The second stack was a record of the times these same schemes were tried and the results. It named the politicians and court officers who had been implicated in corruption cases who were handling the type of transactions.

All of his references were carefully footnoted and sources identified and authenticated. He went to the net to check on the present whereabouts and information on all of them.

Interesting! It seemed there had been three recent deaths among them, including the judge who had declared Forbes persona non grata.

Judge Valdores. He died in a "suspicious" accident. He fell off a third story balcony at his home, landing on the concrete lip of his swimming pool.

Arturo Javeneros M., the person who investigated Penceros and Rancheros originally, was killed in a robbery of a petrol station. He had come into the place when the robbery was in progress and was shot in the head. The robbers escaped without getting the cash that was in a safe the men running the station didn't have a combination for.

Amily Teresa Veras had been electrocuted when the cord on her washer was frayed and grounded to the machine. She was the recording secretary for Valdores.

All within the last two months.

Clint carefully documented the cases and referred to the connections. He added the threat Forbes, the one most connected to all three, had made to him and his family, engendering his interest in what the bunch were doing there. He ran the audios from the phone and his recorder into the program. It was a program a man named JK Kiley had made for him. You read until you came to the necessary recording and right clicked on the hyperlink.

He was going to investigate anyone else who died of uncertain circumstances who might have even been peripherally connected to that bunch. Penceros had made a slip when he said there were more than Forbes who had been expelled.

Was Panceros caught in something, as he suggested, and trying to tell Clint a few things?

It was an outside possibility.

The third stack was about the silver and other things in the comarca, and the fact that Penceros had stated they were trying to get an illegal permit and to have the land declared national property. He noted that the process wasn't yet completed. and that they had backdated papers to indicate they were users of the property and that they filed for ROP that was to be purchased from the government to be titled.

He carried one memory stick to Ben and Earl, one would go to his Cusapín house to be held by Nick Storie, and one to CD Grimes to be held in case of his own unavailability to finalize the case for any reason.

He was well aware that he couldn't bring any of this forward for more than a request to investigate, at this point, and that he would have to admit that it was mostly speculation on his part about what they were doing. All he could hope to do at this point was to get Forbes thrown out of the country. That would leave the others to complete the scheme as soon as Clint Faraday died of old age or whatever.

He laid it out to show it was a criminal conspiracy among a small group, and that they made threats and otherwise acted as a unit.

Now to get something that would tie them up in a way the courts would be forced to act. That would be a matter of getting witnesses to any major part of it. It would have to be solidly tied into the criminal conspiracy or they would produce a goat who would get three or four years and they would be able to complete the plan.

Clint wondered how much Forbes was going to get for sitting in a cell for four years. He would then be expelled ... so. He would be expelled instead of prosecuted. That was why he was here. It was why he had gone to the extremes to get attention while Penceros et al were being reasonable businessmen. While Clint and the police and news media concentrated on him, the others would appear to be embarrassed by him, and would be glad that he was expelled because he was making their entirely aboveboard, except for keeping competition unaware that they were working to get a reasonable blah, blah, bullshit, deal done.

They hadn't counted on Clint Faraday getting involved. He had been very quiet for several years, except for the affairs of the comarca ... but this was an affair that involved the comarca.

It involved the comarca in the northern part, where Clint hadn't been active in even more years. That's why Penceros was so shocked to learn Clint knew about the silver. That was one shot in the dark that hit the target dead center!

The one thing they could not survive was publicity. They

didn't think Clint could work that if he didn't have proof of much more than he had. They could still work it with a few corrupt slimeballs that were in the court system. Penceros and, very definitely, Rancheros, would have those contacts set up and ready to go.

He called Juliene. He would be sending the whole thing as it was set up to her personal computer at her home. He didn't want a chance that anyone else would see it. It would tell them he was going after them. It was too soon for that.

"Juli, I'm going to have to solidify the conspiracy part. I want it tied so tight they can't get past that one point. It's the only weak link in that chain! Conspiracy will tie them all to the same anchor chain.

"Do I sound obsequious or what?

"Forbes has to be connected through conspiracy or their scheme might work – except I guaran-damned-tee you they will have every Ngobe in Panamá gunning for them. That will mean bringing in the police, which would bring international publicity that would force Panamá to act against them.

"I don't want it to come to that.

"Damn it! I'm getting too old for this shit!"

"Clint, we have a lot of information in the files about them. I'll dig as deep as I can. Maybe we can come up with more than the unlikelihood they are up to something that's not crooked. If we can tie them together from the time they were in that corruption mess we can add a lot to your case. We have to be able to show a very strong probability. If we can add our own probability to what you're sending we can get it to the point of the fact they're guilty until proven innocent here will act. They can claim one or two, even five things are coincidental. They can't claim ten are!

"If I remember ... Clint! Penceros got a scare because of the terms of him not going to jail if he stayed clean. He almost got caught at that, but it was *Rancheros* who alibied him off the hook! We have a Hell of a connection for the past six years!"

"I love you, Juli! Find anything else and we can tie them all into it! A conspiracy, all are equally guilty!"

"I might have another thing ... Flores. I'm pretty sure there's some connection about a corrupt judge and him. I think maybe ... Rancheros was in on that. Some character named ... Dunstan? Dunworthy?

"Something like that. Another crumby cheap crook you had expelled so Panamá wouldn't have to pay his room and board in the pen for twenty years.

"I'll research it as close as anything I ever did, Clint. Promise! Those crooks are all tied in one way or another. There aren't really that many, so they're forced to form their own clique. We watch that clique and gather a lot of information that we usually can't ever use.

"Sometimes a piece will fit in one area or another."

They chatted for awhile. Clint was frustrated by what he couldn't do anymore. They agreed to keep in touch. Juli suggested they use a code like they did in that case where Clint disguised himself as his "cousin," Jim Hanrady, with any direct contact.

Well, things were going to start moving. Clint just hoped it would be in time to keep it from getting any bigger. He didn't have Marko to gather information the way he used to. Nick and CD were there, but they didn't know enough about Panamanian crooks to do much, plus he wasn't going to involve them in this.

He was going to investigate who else he had expelled from

Panamá as undesirable.

Neil Duncaster? A mobster connection who had helped the world out by hitting four other mob thugs? It seemed likely.

He went into Bocas Town for a good meal, then to some of the places he used to frequent. Only a few of the people he knew well were still around. It had been a few years since he spent any time in Bocas. He much preferred the comarca.

Obilio and Silvestre Smith, a couple of very close Ngobe friends (yes, quite a few of the local Indigenos are named Smith, Taylor, Robinson, Bosman, Trotman and such) he had helped at various times, and who were running a very successful food supply business that Clint, Judi, and Manny had set up, took him to a new Indigeno bar. He had a pleasant night and went back to his house at about one thirty AM.

He was a little drunk. He didn't drink the beers on the comarca, except when he was with special friends.

In the morning he was going to have to start an intense search for information. These four were certainly not the whole bunch in on the scheme. He wanted to tie everyone concerned on that end together. Miss one, it would just be delayed, not stopped.

He intended to see it stopped. He just hoped he would be able to do that. He didn't delude himself about his loss of abilities, at least on the physical end. His mind was still good. He would put it to use.

He was just sitting at the comp when it dinged. E mail from Juliene:

Clint - Pablo Aristes, Mexico, Mob. Connected to Flores. Rancheros dismissed a case against him four years ago when he was caught in a land scam in Veraguas.

So. The thot plickens.

Clint went through the old files on the comp to bring up Aristes. It seemed he was tied up with a Colombian and a Venezuelan in some kind of deal with that Costa Rican (Book 31: *Rest in Pieces*) woman. Laundering, mostly. He didn't know (or care) what the involvement was – until now.

He went on the police net to look up the case. Aristes was into various scams and laundering. He had connections to a Colombian named Quiroz, who died in a vendetta in Medellin. They were into smuggling emeralds out of the country. They were caught by Interpol. Quiroz died before he could be called to testify. Typical.

Clint sat back. He was getting a headache, and he never did. He found some aspirin in the medicine cabinet and took a couple. It was probably the different food and stress.

Someone called, "Buenos!" at the front door. He glanced at the spy cam picture on the top of the screen, thought a second, turned on the surveillance system and called, "Pase! Está en la cocina!" (Come in! I'm in the kitchen!)

Penceros and Flores came in a moment later. Clint had put Spider Solitaire on the screen and moved a couple of cards before he looked up.

"Oh! I was expecting someone. What's up?"

"We were passing and wanted to speak with you about a few things," Penceros answered. "I don't know if you know Enrique Flores?"

"We've met. What kind of things?"

"Mr. Faraday," Flores replied, "We are caught in a trap of our own making. Had we known you might become involved we would not have built the trap, but it is done and can't be undone.

"We are planning to mine some ores that are on the comarca, if only a very short distance from national land. We planned to have the area declared national land that was open for ROP possession. We have already made most arrangements, and are in possession on the records, if not in actuality.

"Mr. Faraday, it is in a part of the comarca that no one is using, and that no one would be using for many years, if ever. It harms no one, and we would compensate the people there.

"Enrique suggested that we come here to explain. He says you are concerned for the damage to the comarca and the Ngobe. This does no harm. We will restore the land when we have mined the ores. That will be on the contract.

"Other partners, the ones with the power, do not see it that way. They have always taken what they want. This would be no different. They will try to take the land through the planned method. They would agree to only a small compensation to the people of the comarca.

"We are in the trap because of our involvement with those people in the past. We can't escape and live. It is that simple.

"Mr. Faraday, this would not harm the people of the comarca."

"You're both lawyers. You both know perfectly damned well what a precedent is. It would establish a precedent in law that would become a major taking of comarca land. Don't try to hand me a line of BS that a ten year old could see through."

"Mr. Faraday ... I know that would seem to be so, but we will make it a special case exception that could not be used in such a manner," Penceros insisted.

So! That's what they want! A precedent that would destroy the comarca over the years!

"A precedent would be the foot in the door," Clint argued. "Once there, it would always be there.

"Ain't gonna happen while I'm alive to stop it!"

"Then maybe there's another solution to our problem?" Flores hissed.

Clint pulled his Glock from under the computer slide. "Works from either direction, would you say?

"I was planning to go back to Cusapín tomorrow, after the doctors' report. I think maybe I won't!"

Penceros was aghast. "Dios mio! What is the matter with you, Juan Luis!? Dios mio! Mr. Faraday! I swear! I'm no part of any such thing! Dios mio!"

"Penceros, I tend to believe you – to an extent. The extent that you never dreamed I would get involved.

"I am, as of this moment, involved. All the way.

"You can't get out, but your value is not here anymore. If anything ... untoward happens to you, it will involve the policia. It will also involve a lot of publicity, which is the one thing your little scheme can't stand up to. It will bring the Ngobe into it to the point none of your partners had ever be anywhere without a dozen or so bodyguards.

"Penceros, get out of Bocas. I would suggest Panamá City is as close as you should ever come until this is resolved."

"I guess that's our only choice, now," Flores said dejectedly.

"I said Penceros. You threatened me. That makes it personal. I give no corner to the rest of you."

"You don't know who you're dealing with!" Flores cried.

"If Aristes and Duncaster are as good as you can do, you're a thousand kilometers out of your league."

Both Penceros and Flores looked like they'd been kicked in the crotch.

"I suppose you have better ... helpers," Flores said, with a sick attempt at a sneer.

"Bocinni? Armakov? You would ask?"

"Dios mio! I warned them! Dios mio!" Penceros cried.

"You're out of it for now. Keep it that way," Clint said to him, then turned to Flores. "You were leaving."

Flores and Penceros left. Clint was damned glad he had that system on! Here was a video of Flores making a threat on his life!

"That's going to smack you in your obsequious puss!" Clint mumbled.

He ran the video/audio surveillance onto a memory stick and made the three copies. He put the copy for the records into the safe.

"If I have to walk up and blow the brains out of every one of you, so be it!" he said to the wall. "I'm over seventy five. The police can hold me no longer than four hours.

"They can put me under house arrest, but my house is in Cusapín. Even if they can make it here, who cares? If I go to the comarca I'm no longer under Panamanian law.

"I have options you never considered!

"I'm hungry and talking to myself. Shit!"

He went into the kitchen to warm up some lobster chowder from the freezer.

Things were going to get more interesting now. They would figure he wouldn't go after Forbes, so their distraction wouldn't work. That didn't leave a lot of options open for them.

He had to keep them thinking he knew a lot more than he did. Manny was in the Med and Tony simply didn't have the savvy of the old mob connections. Armakov, he didn't want involved. The Russian mafia were not people you could figure in critical times. They were, to Clint's way of thinking, a long way from sane, though Vasily and Ivan were far more reasonable than many.

If he had to, he had to. Whatever it takes.

He warmed up a double portion of frozen chili and sat on the deck to think and eat. He was tired. Part of getting older. A few years ago he could go at this pace for weeks on end.

Another sign of age. "When I was younger...."

Too bad there wasn't an alternative that appealed to him.

He called Tyna and talked for half an hour or so. Judi heard the name, "Carlos Selasia" mentioned in conjunction to Rancheros. She didn't know if it meant anything.

"It damned well could! He was in some kind of scheme to consolidate crime syndicates in Central and South America," (Book 52: *Killer Deal*) Clint replied. "Shit! There were people from several countries involved in that mess!"

It looked like things would get a lot further than interesting. Try scary as Hell on for size!

Clint was wondering how deep this crap went. He also had to wonder what it was really about. A silver lode worked with some of the people involved, but Selasia brought in a whole new perspective.

He would not be involved in a silver mine, real or scam.

Clint sat at the computer to get in touch with Manny. He no longer had the connection with Interpol.

Armakov did not like Selasia. not even a little bit. Maybe he would have some information. It had been eight years since they had any contact, but they got along well.

He asked if Manny had kept an eye on Selasia. Did he know what he was up to?

Clint: Selasia is in a bad spot with Habenaria (Mex) and Marks (Argentina) at the moment. He wouldn't be involved in anything that might bring his name up. His bout with Rancheros was over a deal where he was caught with forty or so cases of contraband cigarettes brought in through Costa Rica. He bought his way out. Rancheros was the judge who dropped the case for insufficient evidence. That they had forty cases of contraband seized from a truck owned by Selasia, with petrol chits signed by him, being delivered to a warehouse owned by him, with two witnesses who testified he gave them money to be given to Mendez, a tobacco dealer in C.R. wasn't sufficient evidence in a country where you are guilty until proven innocent. I have this lovely swamp in a garbage dump I'll sell cheap!

It was a dead end. A coincidence.

Wasn't it?

Clint looked up Vasily Armakov's number and called.

Vasily was in the hospital, critical. Heart. Ivan, his brother answered.

"Clint, Selasia's cut out of anything anymore. He's a mouth-running pain in the ass punk. He gives you any shit, let me know. Tomorrow, no Selasie, so no problem."

"Thanks, Ivan. If he's not involved in whatever the Hell Pencerous and Rancheros are doing, I couldn't care less what else he's into."

"Penceros? That schumpth in Fronterra?"

"Yeah. He's with a group, not by his own choice, if you believe him, that's trying to steal some Ngobe land."

"That silver mine thing? We looked at it. Not likely any deal can be made with the comarca. That museum in Soloy brings in more than anything other than the canal. They can't buy anybody on the comarca, so they won't ... Rancheros.

"They gonna grab the land through the court?"

"They plan to try."

"Then they have backing. If you can find that, you can stop it. Maybe. If you don't, it won't end."

"What I'm afraid of. I want to tie the backing to them and get the whole bunch. I don't have forever anymore."

"Yeah. I'm just celebrating my seventy fourth. You're even more ancient.

"I'll see what I can find. I don't think it's anyone from Panamá, which could mean trouble."

"Thanks, Ivan."

They chatted a minute about things, then Clint rang off.

If Selasia was out of it, it was probably not from Central or South America. Maybe Mexico, maybe the states.

He had to get information, and he had to get it in a way they wouldn't know about it. Only one person he knew could do that.

He called Judi.

They talked about it. Most of the group were in Frontera and David. Chiriqui. He would have to go there to find out where the information might be. He was *not* going to Panamá City!

They made a plan. It would be a lot like old times.

James Arnaz, a man who looked a lot like Clint Faraday – except he was heavier and sported a moustache and walked with a slight hitch, and slowly, gave the butt of the Cuban cigar a disgusted look and tossed it into the gutter in front of the pawn shop where he had just pawned a stereo system for a tenth of its value. He went to the Ciudad de David Hotel to ask if he had received any mail. They explained (for the fourth time) that he would have to pick it up in General Delivery at the post office.

He sighed and went out to walk the five blocks to the post office. He went to the window where people were mailing things, where he was told to go to the window by the door. He went there to ask if there was any mail for James Arnaz.

There was a registered letter. He had trouble with Spanish, but was able to show his passport and stamp, so he got it.

It contained a cashier's check for ten thousand dollars.

He went across the street to Banistmo bank. They would cash it, but he had to wait three days for it to clear, seeing it wasn't issued from a Panamanian bank.

"CitiBank is in Panamá!" he complained. The door guard told him where the CiutiBank branch was, so he walked another six blocks to get to the CitiBank. They cashed the check and warned him not to carry that kind of cash around.

He didn't have anywhere else to put it.

"You say you are staying at the Ciudad de David? They have a safe for their clients."

He took a taxi to the hotel, deposited the cash in the safe, went next door to the pawn shop and got his stuff back. It cost him twenty bucks for two hours. Shit!

He put the stereo in his room and went to the restaurant, saw it was too early to eat, so went to his room to watch TV.

His Indio friend, who worked in the restaurant, said the only people who seemed the kind he was looking for ate early, then went out on the town every night. They had been there for more than a month. They ate in other restaurants sometimes, but usually were there on Monday and Tuesday nights. They would be in the restaurant at about 6:00.

Mae Matisu went to the desk to ask if her cousin had left a message. She was handed a note, read it, and rolled her eyes at the ceiling.

"Mal noticias?" the desk girl asked. "Oh! You speak some English and almost no Spanish.

"Bad news?"

"I think not so, but probably maybe yes. She has gone to where she went so not to be here so sorry."

"Well, those things happen."

"Maybe it so for real with life being a crap shoot!"

"I speak Mandarin," the bellboy said, in Mandarin.

"So do I!" she replied. "I am from the islands, but my parents taught me Mandarin and Cantonese.

"My cousin was supposed to meet me here. She has to be in a comarca or whatever they call it. I guess I'll have to try to get by on my own. It will be an adventure!"

"There is a woman staying here who speaks the trade language and Mandarin. She s with some people from the

United States, but she is Panamanian. They will be in the dinning room at about six or six thirty. If I see you both I will introduce you."

"Oh! Thank you! It will be good to meet other people with whom I can communicate!"

She chatted a moment, then went up to her room. She got on the elevator with Arnaz and two others. Arnaz said, "Three." She said, "Oh! It is to speak the English I can but not too much sometimes. I am Mae."

"Yeah. Not many speak English here and my Spanish smells. I'm Jim, from Oregon."

"Is in Canada?"

"No. The US."

"I was in the US, but only in New York. It is to not like city so big. No people are real."

"I feel the same about New York!"

"Well and good! Maybe it is to meet two who are people today and can communicate some a little!"

She got off on two. Clint went on up to three.

She said, in their code, that there was someone else who she could communicate with. What did she mean?

Clint sat at a table to the side and sat reading the menu, ordered a red wine, and studied the list. He really would like local food, but had to stay in character, so ordered a 16 ounce ribeye.

He looked around the room. There were only four others there. It was early. He had the ability to look at things to the side of where he seemed to be looking. His peripheral vision was far more than most.

Several people came in in the next twenty minutes. He was served, and found the steak to be very good.

The group he was waiting for came in. It was several people he'd met on a case. (book 52: *Killer Deal*) who would be, if connected, bad news. This was the group involved with Selasie.

He had to know if they were connected. He did know they were up to no good if they were involved with anything at all. He was a little worried about Judi. She had met them all in a restaurant in Marioto.

She was in disguise there, too. Not this one.

Judi knew. The comment about two who could communicate was because one of them spoke the trade dialect in Chinese.

Judi carried a broadcasting device. Thankfully, it wasn't the same type as before.

Eight years. Probably safe enough.

The group sat at a table toward the center front. Judi came in and walked by them, not even seeming to glance at them. She took a nearby table, not too far from them.

They ordered. The waiter went to Judi, whose mangled Spanish didn't seem good enough to get through to him. She tried English, which she mangled even worse.

Inez Marinera, the woman in the group, called something in Chinese. Judi replied with a slight bit of difficulty. Inez spoke in Mandarin. Judi answered in Mandarin.

Inez invited Judi to join them, explaining to the group that she hadn't had a chance to practice her Chinese in five years. Judi came to the table where she was introduced to the group, to which she answered in English. "Mae Matisu. You're welcome and thanks a million times. Very good morning to you all!"

Inez started chatting in Mandarin. Judi did her airhead act. They all ordered beverages, and Inez said, in English, that they had ordered the sizzling shrimp dinner.

"Is funny too good! I come to halfway in the ocean and would to eat favorite food from home! Very good wonderful is it!"

"You can tell us if it is really as good and authentic as they claim!" Inez replied. Judi looked lost, so she repeated in Mandarin.

They chatted happily for the truly excellent meal. Clint couldn't very well sit there much longer, so signed the check and went out. Inez looked at him studiously as he passed and said something to Fred Benson. He said he didn't think so. Judi smiled at him as he passed. Inez said something to Judi, who answered.

They ignored him, after that. He went to his room to try to listen to what Judi was doing.

Judi went to the restaurant. They were sitting at a table near the center. Clint was to the left, a few tables away. She took a fairly close table and acted totally confused with the waiter. Inez Martinera, who she'd met (though Inez didn't know that) in Mariato, interpreted for her, as she had planned. She was invited to their table.

Inez chatted with her in Mandarin about where she was from and what she came to Panamá for. She said from an island near the China coast, and that she wanted to see the world. She had a cousin who ran a little store in a place called Chiriqui. She was supposed to meet her, but she had been called away for business or something, so here she was, not being able to talk to many.

She was introduced to the other three people, who she knew by sight. They were all involved in the Mariato case.

Clint passed by. She smiled at him.

"Oh? Do you know that man?" Inez asked.

"I spoke to him in the elevator. He seemed nice, but was a little grumpy."

"He looks like a man I knew seven or eight years ago. Clint Faraday."

"His name is Jim Something."

"Hanrady?" Inez seemed very interested, so they knew about one of Clint's disguises.

"Arnite or something. Nitex? Arnaz! He's Jim Arnaz, I think he said. From Canada."

"Oh. Jim Hanrady was from Texas."

They changed the subject. Inez would chat for a minute in Mandarin, then would talk to the men in Spanish and English.

The meal was delicious. She said it wasn't like at home. It was better!

Judi took a worked silver and turquoise compact from her purse, then said she didn't know if Panamá was like New York, where she couldn't look at her face at the table, or like back home, where she could.

It contained the sending microphone, very much miniaturized.

Inez knew about the technology. She said it was a truly beautiful compact, and asked to look at it. Judi handed it to her. She opened it and found face powder.

"It was a gift from a man I met. A beautiful man. In a place called La Mina (Very close to the silver lode). I spent a night at his home. He was a very good lover! We communicated, but had no words. It didn't matter," Judi explained. "He made the compact for me. He said there was a lot of silver and turquoise there close."

"He was Latino?" Inez asked.

"No. He was what they call an Indio. An indigenous person."

"La Mina? I hear there is some silver there," Benson said, in English. "It's on the comarca, so only the Indios can get it."

"What?" Judi replied. "It is from there close but not too far. He say it Bugle so he use want whatever but not to other for not Nawbigee or something."

"Then it is on the comarca and can't be mined," Estevez said, in Spanish. "Not enough there to bother with, probably. There are always stories of a find that's got to be the biggest in history or something on the comarca. You can get in on it for ten thousand dollars, but only today, because somebody else offered that much. Probably a small lode. Not worth the trouble, but you can make a deal with the man to bring it to you for a price.

"I never did believe any of the stories. They're always a big dream that doesn't happen."

They chatted more, but silver or the comarca or mines didn't come up again. Inez talked about a deal to import liquor, at times. Benson always changed the subject.

This bunch wasn't involved. Clint would be happy about that.

Judi finally said she was going to her room. She had to go to Tolé in the morning, then to Bocas, then back home. She asked what her part of the check was. Benson said they invited her, so they would pay the tab. She was very good company. It was too bad they couldn't speak with her directly. She was a very interesting and attractive person.

She did the blushing innocent act and left.

"They're out of it," she said to the compact in the elevator.

Clint nodded at the compact, cleaned up, and went to bed. He would still have to find who was financing that bunch and be able to tie it.

"Clint? Tony here.

"You asked to find who was involved with the silver lode. I can't say for sure, but the name John Horvath has come up once too often. He's been in touch with your whole group."

"I never heard of him."

"He's CEO and president of an investment company, on the board of a large drug company, and has a financing project totally in his own name. Out of Houston. Word is that he snacks on sharks for kicks.

"He financed a couple of movies that made a bundle. Those special effects James Bond ripoff things.

"He's a do-it-yourself type who thinks he can do a thing better than you because he's smarter than you."

"In other words, a greedy millionaire with no morals or ethics."

"Sorta. Billionaire. Four, all but five or six million in assets. Five million in cash is enough to squeak by."

"Yeah. I'm down to that, but it will, as you say, get you by.

"Any chance he would come to Panamá?"

"He goes to San Blas at times. He goes to PC at times. He has even gone to David. He's in Seattle, at the moment. Has his own private transportation.

"Clint, he might have a tie-in with some people you've come across before. A Faith Somebody who was into a sick hunter game?"

"Faith Richards?" (book 9: *Follow the Blood*)

"Uh-huh."

"Totally emotionless. If he's that sort, this ain't gonna be any fun.

"Thanks, Tony. Horvath may be the only name I need. I have to tie him into it and get him here."

They chatted about the projects, then rang off. Clint sat back, thought, and tried a roaming number in the states that worked ten years ago.

It worked!

"Faith? Clint Faraday here. Remember me?"

"Certainly! How are things, Clint? How are you still alive, as many people as you've had after your ass."

"They can't get to me on the comarca. After awhile, they don't see any reason. I do what I do, they did what they do. There are consequences. That's life."

"Too true! What do you want? Surely you're not calling all the people you know from the past to chat."

"No fooling you! What do you know about a John Horvath?"

"Lousy in bed. Doesn't feel anything and hasn't learned to fake it – like the rest of us. My psycho – logical group."

"I've told him about you. Surely he hasn't gotten in touch with you?

"He wouldn't.

"He might. You'd be a challenge."

"He's into something here that is going to stop. It can hurt a lot of people who *do* feel. Deeply. Me included."

"What can I do – or is this just to confirm what you knew about him?"

"Unless you can tell me how to get him to come to Panamá, it's just for information."

"What'll you do? Blow his brains out? You have to be a hundred by now. Can you handle it?"

"I'm getting awful close to a hundred. If blowing his

brains out is the only way, it's the only way."

"I might be able to get him there. I'd like to see you again. Is the promise I would never go to Panamá again still in effect?"

"No. You're an exception. I think you're not a bad person. I didn't always think that way.

"You would get him to come here knowing he might get his brains smeared all over the sidewalk?"

"Sure! Remember how I met you? I might find it amusing. I do feel a minor amusement, at times.

"Clint, John likes to think he's smarter than anyone else. He'll go to extremes to prove it. I think I ... how about if I get him, not only to Panamá, but onto the comarca?"

"Could you do that?"

"I think so. I'll offer him a challenge. I'll make him think he's outsmarting the whole damned world! I'll put it to him that there's something that the best criminal minds in the world worked on and failed. He won't be able to resist that!"

They chatted about old times for awhile. She promised she would get Horvath to Panamá – by telling him it might be a one-way trip. He would accept the challenge. He might, as Faith had done, finally find a moment of actual feeling. A thrill.

Clint then sat at the computer and listed everything new they had found. He listed a lot of things that he suspected in a form he could check whether they were true or false conclusions.

He was getting another headache. This crap was getting to him a lot more than he wanted to admit. He was too used to the tranquil life on the comarca. He just wanted this to be over.

"Where are we?" Judi asked. "Any closer to getting it resolved?"

"I think I have a lever. I think I know who's behind it. I might have a way to finish it, but have to depend on a woman whose psychology I simply can't understand."

"Well, Tyna said to make sure you keep the promise to see the doctor today for the followup."

"Judi, I want you out of this. It can get a lot more dangerous than you know. There's going to be a person coming after me who I can't figure. He's known to be a totally cold fish. Tony says he snacks on sharks for amusement."

"I've learned to take your advice. I'm out of it. I won't mention it again unless I happen on something I think you should know."

"Fair enough.

"Judi, if ... I want you to explain to Tyna that I'm in something I have no control over. If anything happens to me, I expected it. You don't have to say she was never off my mind from the moment we were married. Never. She and the kids are my first priority, always were, and always will be. She knows that."

"Clint ...?"

"I may not survive this one, Judi. You know I've always loved you as my best friend. If anything happens ... my family. You're part of my family. We all feel that way."

They were silent for a moment, then Judi nodded her agreement.

"Clint, what's the matter? Really?"

"Judi, I've never had a headache, except when I'd been smacked or something, in my entire life. Now I have a constant one.

"The doctors found a spot in an inoperable part of my brain. They don't think it's serious.

"I think it's serious.

"If I get to where I can't think straight, tell ... no. Call Manny and say to wipe that bunch off the face of the Earth, if it's not over by then. All the information and proof is in the memory stick I'll give you. It will be in the recipes, like before."

"Clint...."

"We have to be realistic and we have to be prepared."

She nodded. She reached to touch him. He stood and held her for a long moment. No further words were necessary.

When Judi went back to her house Clint went to the hospital for the doctor to tell him things seemed normal enough. He could tell by the evasions that the doctors had found that things were *not* normal enough.

"Doc, I have an inoperable tumor of the brain. Surely you don't think I can't handle the truth?"

"We don't know enough yet. It my remiss, or it may not. It won't affect you much. You'll get sleepier and sleepier, then one morning you won't wake up. About two months, if it's fast, three if not."

"Can you stop the headaches?"

"Yes, to a fairly great extent. I'll give you what we have here and a prescription you can get refilled as much as you feel is necessary. If you overdose it will affect your reaction time and leave you confused. You have to decide on the level that works for you."

He got the rest of the information, thanked the doctors, and went into town to see what was new. It was late enough for dinner, so he went to the Lemon Grass for some Thai food.

The food was very good, but things were just not the same.

He remembered when he and Judi and Tyna would come to
see their nutty friend, Dave, play with the local talent in the
band. All 60's and 70's music, except for the odd request or
something one of them wrote.

He went to the golden Grill, but that wasn't the same,
either.

Don't get depressed. Not on top of everything else.

He went out a ways to the Indio bar he had come to often
in the past. Guilermo was there with Silvio and Obilio. They
had a good time.

Then he went home to bed.

The sunrise was beautiful. All golds and pinks. The 1/4
moon was just above the horizon, with small fleecy clouds
here and there close, and a glowing pink band just above.
Carenero on the horizon, making a dark line between the
clouds and water, where the reflections of the colors on the
bay were like floating flower petals.

How could such a beautiful serene scene exist in a world
with the most disgusting sleaze in control of too many
things?

There was nothing to do but wait – but not for long. His
time, for the first time in his life, had definite limits.

Clint wondered if the cancer cure Dave had learned about
in time to cure a lesion on his forehead would work on what
he had. That one worked on prostate cancer, Dave had tried
it for the lymphoma and it had worked. He had tried to get
it known, but was thwarted by the drug companies, who
would lose their lucrative chemotherapy market.

What was the plant? Artemisia?

Yes. It also cured leishmaniasis, a scourge second only to
malaria. It was almost a weed, in places, but no one knew

about it, and news about it was silenced.

In the name of profits.

Don't get into that shit now. You have to keep yourself away from depression. That's vital!

He went inside for his first cup of coffee, then swam off the deck for awhile.

The rest of the day was on the computer and moving around Bocas Town, talking to old friends, half of whom were glad the touristiest parts were now concentrated at Drago, and half of whom cried about the lost money when the tourists didn't stay there.

Same anywhere in the "civilized" world. Liberal and conservative ideas. Clint was glad the terms didn't really apply to comarca life.

The next day was a repeat. He was holding his own with the headaches, and found they were slightly less.

The next day started the same, then he got a call. Faith Richards. She said she and a man from the states, a man called John, were flying into Panamá in about four hours. John had always wanted to see the pirate ship at Soloy (book 51: *Dead Man Talking*) and she could use a vacation. They might run into him there, or in David. They were going to make a week or more out of the trip.

So! She came through! He was actually going to go to the comarca! He was going to try to find a way to steal the artifacts in the museum. That was the thing no master criminal had been able to do. In fact, four had been caught and had been executed. Comarca law demanded that anyone caught taking anything from the museum was to be executed. Period. No mitigating circumstances. No technicalities. They were stealing from the comarca. Anyone stealing from the comarca was to be executed. Next case!

Could he get the rest of the bunch onto the comarca? Comarca law could end this scheme in a very final manner.

No. Horvath was keeping his name out of it.

There had to be a way to connect them. It would then be a matter of conspiracy, all the way.

Faith would bring Horvath to the comarca. She wouldn't do more. It was up to Clint to figure what he would do, and to counter it. That was part of the game, to her.

Could he do that?

He simply didn't know enough about Horvath. He would have to go on psychology.

So. He had easy access to drugs. He could try to drug someone. He thought he was clever. He would be the type to ... he financed those movies. He might try some of that phony technological crap. They depended on a place being closed for the master criminal to be able to use the gadgets.

The museum never closed. What would be his options?

Clint called Silvio, who was the manager of the pirate ship museum. Every six hours the separate sections were closed for half an hour for the cleaning crew.

"Well, Mr. Horvath! Surprise, surprise!"

Clint called Penceros and said he was going to be in Soloy for a day or two. He would then go back to Bocas Town. It might be unwise for him to be in Bocas Town when Clint got back. Penceros said he had no intention of ever going to David or Bocas again.

Clint smirked and called for his special helicopter pilot he hadn't used in more than three years to pick him up and take him to Soloy. Luckily the chopper was free for a few hours.

"Let's get this boat in the water – or chopper in the air – or something as trite!"

Clint went directly to the museum, where he was greeted warmly by many of his friends. Silvio was getting old now, but was still a powerful man. He had a very sharp mind and a wonderful sense of humor.

Clint explained that this man was behind a plot to steal Ngobe land. The silver was important to it in that it was used to set a precedent in the courts that would haunt the Ngobe until they had nothing left, unless it was stopped now. It was also something to educate the Ngobe about the methods that would be tried in the future, when there was no Clint Faraday to discover the plots.

"What this man will do is try to steal things from the museum. He feels he is smarter than a bunch of savages, but he also knows the risks he'll be taking. He knows he faces success or death.

"Silvio, he doesn't feel. If he loses, he will say, 'That's the way it goes!' He may have a slight fear that his execution will be painful, but that is all."

"We do not torture, even in a psychological sense, unless a situation arises where it is necessary. That is for the so-called civilized world. He will be executed, not held for years with a little hope, then a ceremony where he is strapped to a table or into a chair with time to fear and hope there will be a reprieve, which is an extension of the torture, no more.

"We will not have a crew of very expensive lawyers getting rich, and preachers and social workers keeping the family in a state of mental torture, or newsprint and television milking it for those years.

"He will be tried, convicted, and executed in a matter of a few hours, if the evidence is there. Next case. That has been made clear to the entire world."

"Exactly what I planned."

"You set him up? We will have to consider that, Clint! You know that! It would be using the Ngobe, though it would be to our advantage to stop this."

"No, Silvio. I think you know me better than that. It was suggested by another, a person very much like him. All I've done is point out that no one has ever been smart enough to steal from the museum. The four who tried are dead. Executed.

"Another person even suggested that. He knows the risks exactly. It is how he thinks. He's totally empty of emotions. He has made himself into a billionaire, meanwhile learning money and power are empty, yet he continues. It's a basic death wish. We'll be the vehicle that delivers his wishes. He knows that one day he'll fail.

"Silvio, he has no emotions, no feelings. It will be like turning off a misprogrammed computer."

"Yes. I have met the type. He will figure he screwed that one up. Sad. Pass the yuca, please."

They decided to let Horvath make the plan, they would observe, it would end – if he was stupid enough to actually try to steal from the museum.

"It will be something small, just to prove he was smart enough to do it," Silvio suggested.

Clint shook his head. "It will be physically small, but something that will be noticed soon. He can't gloat if no one knows about it."

"We will see what he plans and how clever he actually is. He cannot buy his way out of it here. We have more than ninety billion dollars in the bank for the people. I think he cannot bribe anyone here!"

"He'll try to do it himself. Buying his way out of it might come later, but he'll have failed by then."

Silvio nodded and sighed.

Clint watched as the private jet landed in David. Faith and Horvath got off and went to the Ciudad de David, where they booked the penthouse. Clint kept them in view.

His cellular buzzed. He answered.

"Hi, Clint! Faith Richards here! I came to David with a friend who wants to see more of Panamá. He's been here before, but wants to see the pirate ship at Soloy. Pictures don't show much.

"Could you arrange anything so he doesn't have to do the tour bit?"

"No. I don't have any pull there. He doesn't have to go along with the tour. He can go as an independent student of history and wander around all he wants. I can probably arrange a special price, or that he not be restricted to the time he spends there."

"It's a hundred dollars an hour. He's paid for ten hours, and can go tomorrow. I'll go for maybe an hour. I'd like to see it.

"Are you in David?"

"Close."

"Dinner tonight? You know the best places. I'll introduce you to John."

"You went to the better places when you were here. I don't get into David much anymore. I'm not up to date."

"What was the name of that open air place with the great shrimp and sizzlers? Typical or something?"

"La Tipica?"

"I liked their food, and it was a nice enough place. I don't like the overdone fancy snobbery places.

"There? Seven?"

"Okay. Sounds good to me."

"We'll catch up then! John wants to wander around town a little. I'll shop. See you tonight!"

They rang off. Clint went to the Alcalá for a room.

Maybe tonight he would learn what Horvath planned, though it wouldn't be necessary. He wasn't going to be out of sight for a second. There were a lot of Indios in David. It wouldn't be necessary to have just one or two followers for Horvath to spot.

They had as many as needed. Horvath wasn't going to see the same one too often.

"Clint! I almost didn't recognize you! I thought you were in your eighties. You look like your sixties."

"Hi. Faith. I'm ninety in two months. You're as stunning as you were. Glad to see you don't play the bimbo game anymore."

"A bimbo running two corporations doesn't play, and I'm as much older as any of us.

"This is John Horvath. Clint Faraday."

"The famous detective. I've heard a lot about you, mainly from Faith." Horvath said.

"I remember reading something about you. Head of a very successful corporation or something. I don't keep up with that stuff. I live on the comarca and live like the natives, for the most part."

Faith laughed. "Clint has a few million in the bank and works like the Indios. He digs yuca and cuts timber and all that."

"I'm Ngobe. I live like my people."

"Yes. You were declared Ngobe. I heard about that," Horvath replied. "I'm far too spoiled to ever want to do physical labor.

"I don't know, though. You're ninety? You could pass for sixty five, easily. People like me look ninety when they're sixty five, not vice versa."

"It's good genes and keeping fit." They chatted, had a delicious meal, then went to Peter's bar. Horvath said he was going to Soloy the following day to study some at the pirate ship museum. Could he get a flight, or would he have to take a bus?

"You flew in, Faith said. Didn't they tell you the landing strip at Soloy is better than Malek?"

"I flew in my own plane. I didn't know I could go there directly!"

"A flight there and back, twice a day. Lots of Europeans and a lot of North Americans fly there, directly," Clint explained. "You have to get reservations for the field. It's full a lot of the time. I can call Silvio, the director, and see if they have space.

"What kind of aircraft?"

"Lear executive twelve."

Clint took out his cellular and called Silvio. A plane was leaving later tonight. The next one due wasn't reserved specifically for tomorrow. Horvath could come. Clint handed him the phone.

"How much are the fees. I'll bring the cash," Horvath said quickly.

"Fees? Oh, let me see. Medium-sized jet. Eighty five dollars and fifty cents per day.

"We prefer credit cards to cash. It's easier."

"I'll be there at what time?"

"Anytime after six thirty AM."

"Six thirty one!"

"No. Make it six thirty seven!" Silvio returned, with a laugh. "The commercial inflight, you know. No need wasting fuel circling for six minutes."

The rest of the night was pleasant. Horvath was an excellent host, and seemed a very friendly type. Clint could like him if he didn't know it was a facade that was part of the psychology of that group. Horvath, like Faith, was an expert at projecting emotions. In reality, they felt nothing. Being excellent spontaneous actors was a survival trait.

Faith suggested Clint stay with her in her suite.

"Same old me. My wife. Period."

She laughed. "I'm jealous as Hell of the bitch! That's the first turndown I've gotten in ten years!"

They parted. Clint said he might see them in Soloy. He had to go there. They may still be around.

"You can go with us!" Faith cried.

He said it would probably be more comfortable than the helicopter he rode around in.

"You still ride around Bocas on a motorcycle?" Faith asked.

"No. I don't drive. I think it's not smart to drive a car if you're over eighty five. Definitely not a bike."

"We'll see you at five thirty at Malek," Horvath said. "Get up early and be there or we go without you!"

Clint laughed. Faith said she didn't doubt he was always up before five. He was always having his third or forth coffee by then.

Clint soon went to his room and set the alarm for 4:30.

Tomorrow, show time!

The sleek Lear jet made a perfect landing and drew into the open plot where it would stay until they left. Horvath was eager to get directly to the museum. Faith would go for about an hour, then would wander around Soloy. She booked a flight back to David at noon.

Clint went into the museum with them, where the magnificent old pirate ship was sitting on the actual old dry dock cart it had rested on for almost a hundred years before it was brought to Soloy. The silver plated cannon was still in its place, as were the other artifacts in their cases. Swords with jeweled handles, gold doubloons, art works, tapestries, and normal things used on the old ships.

There were rooms where the records and logs from the ship were displayed, and where different kinds of booty from the ship were shown. There were the original videos from when the ship was brought through the canal, the fantastic approach at sunrise with the cloud bank behind and the crew, descendants of the original crew along with Clint and his family and the president and first lady at the time.

Tyna was a spectacular beauty, even among the Ngobe. Horvath said he could see why Clint turned Faith down!

"The problem with the bitch is that she's that good looking and a great person with it! I could stand her if she was like normal people and acted like she pissed champagne and shit ice cream!" Faith complained. "You can't help liking her.

"I heard from several people that your daughter is almost as beautiful, and your son is the sex king of the comarca."

Clint laughed. "He's more like me. He *was* the sex king until he got married. Nicole is a truly beautiful woman."

"Is it true your son was raped when he was eight years

old?" Faith asked innocently.

"Raped? No. He wanted to see what it was like and was with a good friend who was about fourteen, and tried it," Clint replied. "He said it was okay, but not special. The Indios don't look at those things like others."

"Your son tried homosexual relations because he wanted to see what it was like, and told you about it?!" Horvath cried. "I'd think you'd go ballistic!"

"It's part of life. We Ngobe don't try to pretend life is any different than it is. From about thirteen to sixteen or so kids want to experiment. The only difference is that we don't sneak around and lie about it. It doesn't do any damage to them when it's not put on them as a guilt trip. He wanted to know. He found out. He ran around with his special group like kids and teenagers will. I don't doubt for a single second that he tried a lot of things from both ends. I don't doubt that he had special relationships. Big deal!"

"You had a rather wide open life, I guess. I wasn't raised that way," Horvath said.

"To tell the truth, I didn't. I've never had any direct homosexual encounters, though a couple of times I think I would have, even after I became Ngobe.

"If anything had happened to me in the states, I would probably react a lot differently than I do. I would have all kinds of guilt for things I didn't control and would be a different person than I am.

"What I actually felt when Nito told me about it is a lot different than how I acted. I wanted to kill the bastard who screwed my son, but I just asked if he liked it. He said it wasn't special, but he didn't *dis*like it.

"I know it's just life. It's the way it is, not how you want it to be. Fight it, and you're miserable. Accept it, and it doesn't bother you. All it says is that Nito is a normal kid who tries things normal kids try and doesn't feel guilty or try to hide that he's normal.

"If he'd been raped, there would be a dead rapist, and he wouldn't be any different than he is. He would know it wasn't his fault, and he would be stupid to feel guilty about something he had no control over.

"I would kill the rapist. I would have an 'Oh, really? That was wrong. No one has a right to do anything to you that you don't want, but that's life!' He would never know how I felt or how I reacted.

"What the Hell brought this on?"

Faith laughed. "I was pissed that you turned me down and wanted to get in a dig. It backfired, but I had to expect that with you. Back home, telling a man you knew his son had gay relations would make the guy go, as John said, ballistic.

"No more! Let's look around this place. It's fantastic, really."

A man came from the offices with a mop, broom, bucket, and rags. He hung a sign on the door of the records room that said it was closed for one half hour for maintenance.

"I thought the museum never closed!" Horvath said.

"A room at the time. They have to clean them. Each room is closed for a half hour a day, except the main room with the ship. That's closed in small sections that don't interfere with the tours," Clint replied.

"Oh! There's the one I want to see! I'm a woman and all that jewelry is a big draw!" She pointed to the historic artifacts door.

They went in, where there were some hundreds of closed cases with emeralds, rubies, diamonds, opals, sapphires, and others displayed. The first case inside the door had a huge emerald in a solid gold setting with twenty diamonds around it. It's estimated value for the jewels was twelve million nine hundred thousand dollars. It's historical value wasn't possible to appraise.

Clint said he had to get to a meeting, so would leave them to their own devices. He left.

Faith looked around for almost two hours, took a lot of pictures, and left. Horvath stayed for five hours, and would come back the next day for the other five.

Clint didn't see them the rest of the day. He observed Horvath through the system in the museum. Horvath would be surprised at the complete covering of every inch. Everything was recorded.

"Ah! Here he comes!" Silvio said. He and Clint and the four regular operators of the surveillance system were in the security section office. "You say he will try to take something from the jewelry room. It is the fourth cleaned, so he will try then. We will see."

Horvath wandered around until ten minutes before the room would be closed for cleaning. He went into the room and studied it carefully. When the man announced the room would be closed for half an hour, everyone else left. He slipped behind a case, then under it when the man checked. The man went out. Horvath went to a case that held six major artifacts with emeralds as the centerpieces. He took something from his briefcase and quickly opened the lock, took a piece out, and relocked the case.

He went toward the door just as it opened and the cleaning man came in. He slipped behind a case and waited. The man went past. He slipped toward the door. The cleaning man turned and saw him. He moved close and said something.

The man said "No," and shook his head.

Horvath suddenly swung a hypodermic syringe at the cleaning man, who collapsed almost immediately. Horvath headed to the door and opened it – to find Clint, Silvio, and two guards there.

Silvio went to the cleaning man and checked his pulse. He shook his head.

"What was it?" Clint asked.

"Curare."

Clint shot him exactly between the eyes.

"Judge finds him guilty of murder and of theft from the museum. Execution is ordered," Silvio said sadly. "Clint, I never believed for a second he would kill anyone. I never did!"

"I didn't either. He's named as a conspirator, but that isn't proven, to any extent."

"It is on the comarca. Get them here and we end this scheme in a permanent way. This was too much, too far."

Clint nodded. A crew came to take Horvath's body away. Another crew came to take the cleaning man's body out and to return the necklace to the case.

"It would seem our schemers are now one down," Silvio said sadly.

"We have to end this!" Clint snarled. "We can't touch them without the ... clear evidence. All I have now is supposition.

"I don't have time! Damn it, I don't have time!"

"You'll think of a way. You always do. Conspiracy to fraud won't be much, but it will allow us to protect ourselves in the future. We take what we can get. This Horvath was the backing, so it will have to wait for them to get other financing. Perhaps, with it then shown it was a conspiracy to defraud, they will not find other financial help.”

Clint shook his head and said, bitterly, “It’s not enough. All I really have is the threats with supposition about the rest of it.

“I’ll have to think on it.”

Faith Richards came into the office. “I hear Dear John isn’t a problem anymore.”

“Faith, he killed a man,” Clint said. “We never figured he’d do that. It went a lot further than I ever anticipated. I’ll feel guilty about that.”

“I never figured that, either. I thought he’d simply say he tried. No go. Didn’t feel a thing. Shit!

“I’m sorry about your friend. You said you would blow his brains all over the sidewalk. You wouldn’t have done that if he didn’t kill that man, would you?”

Clint thought. “Probably not.”

“I’ll go back home. This is really an interesting place.

“Should I arrange for someone to come after his jet?”

“No,” Silvio answered. “He committed a murder on the comarca. Anything he had on the comarca is now comarca property, and will be given to Edwardo’s family.”

“That seems fair enough,” she replied. “I think I like the law here. No bullshit. Here’s what the law says. That’s the end of it. Go bribe somebody else someplace else.”

“Uh-huh.”

Clint sat at his computer in Bocas Town to bring up all the things he had. It was complete, to his mind, but a court wouldn't consider it except for the threats, which were videotaped and conclusive. Making the threats would get him a restraining order, no more. Unless they were acted on. If they were acted on, it would authenticate most of whatever else he had. Maybe.

This had to end. He wasn't thinking nearly as well as before, and knew it. He simply would not and could not let his people down.

He spent some time considering what he had. He added about Horvath being the backing, and how he had been executed on the comarca for killing a man and stealing from the comarca.

If he brought them up for the threats, would that stop the financing enough? Would it result in not going ahead with the scheme to set a precedent?

No way. He had to have much more serious charges against them.

He sighed and went to the surveillance computer. It would help his case, minimally, that Flores and Forbes were in his house, searching for something. It could be surmised that something was what it actually really was. Evidence against them.

If he caught them in his house after those threats he could defend himself in whatever way seemed advisable. Like a shot between the eyes.

That would get Forbes and Flores out of it, but they weren't the main objective. He probably couldn't tie the whole conspiracy to that. They had it set up to make it look like Forbes and Flores were acting on their own. They would have to do something to make the court have to act on the evidence he supplied. Something a clever lawyer and crooked court system couldn't get around.

He knew one way that would work. One way they would have to use the evidence he'd gathered.

He sighed again and took another pill. The headaches were reduced to a dull background feeling that wasn't really pain, but that wasn't really not pain.

He didn't have long.

He sat at the computer to explain what the doctors found and what he felt. He finished with, "Tyna, I love you more than it is possible to relate. You too, Nito and Nicole. You have all proven to be the kind of people who give me constant pride. If there is an eternity, you will not be forgotten for one second in that time.

"Judi, you have been my truest and best friend since I met you. At times, you were my rock.

"My people, you have given me a life that is full and pleasant. You have given me a philosophy to not fight nature, but to join with it.

"Sergio, Silvio – all my friends on and off the policia, I love you with a never-ending pride of having you in my life.

"I am not going to be around long. I do not want you to grieve for me. I want you to know joy in that I was inspired by you all, that you gave me a wonderful life that leaves me without regrets. I am not a good man, and not a bad man. I am me.

"Nick and Janet and CD and Alma, you have become very special friends who I know will help my people and my family at anytime you are needed. Pancho, you know you are included in that

"I will finish this later. My pills are making me groggy and confused. I just want this recorded for when I can no longer say what must be said.

"Nito, protect the comarca and our people. I know you will."

He turned the audio off, but left the video running.

He went into Bocas Town and to the Reef, where Naldo said Flores and Forbes were meeting. He went to their table to say their financing seemed to be in jeopardy.

"So. You set a man up so you can shoot him. Maybe he wasn't our only source," Forbes snarled. "You'd better watch your back, Faraday. Remember. What goes around comes around."

"Ah! I see you got the point! I'll get the records I need in the next day or two and your little scheme will end – *then* you get sent back to the states and will *not* come back to Panamá again!"

"Er, records?" Rancheros asked.

"You can't hide from your past with anyone who knows how to find things comes into it. It's what I do. I've got some things you thought were buried.

"Guess what! They've been dug up.

"When I add them to what I already have, you're gone. All of you.

"Enjoy your meal. I hear prison food doesn't quite make the five star gourmet standards you wish to become accustomed to." He turned and walked away.

Now to see if they would do what he felt they would.

He went back to the house to set up a little device on his deck. He straightened some things and washed all the dirty dishes.

He sat to make a short recording, then called Judi, who was, as he knew, in Changuinola. He asked her to bring some of the sour cream they had in Romero's there. He couldn't get it in Bocas or Almirante.

There was a call from in front. He switched on the surveillance system and said to come on in. He was at the computer.

Forbes and Flores came in with, as he had hoped, Rancheros in tow.

They argued about a few things. He baited Forbes into following his nature and making some threats, including him getting a bullet through the head like he had done to Horvath.

He ordered them out of his house.

He then went to the deck to sit at the little table there with a cup of coffee. He switched on the recorder at the place where he left off.

He positioned himself exactly and pushed a piece of coat hanger wire he had been making holding clips for the orchids from onto a hook affair on the railing on the deck over the water.

"... death by murder of well known detective, Clinton Faraday, Ngobe by declaration.

"Detective Faraday was working on a case where a fraudulent scheme to steal Indigeno property on the comarca Ngobe Bugle was exposed. The principles of the case were in his home, where his secret security system recorded an argument in which one of those people threatened to shoot him between the eyes. It seems the threat was carried out. Clint, as his friends called him, was shot between the eyes only a very few moments later.

"The security video/audio recorder showed that one of those people came back and shot Clint, then threw to pistol into the sea. Police have recovered the weapon.

"Here is special detective Geraldo Herrera of the Policía Nacionál, who is investigating the case."

"Thank you, Pamela.

"I was trained by Capitan Sergio Valdez, ironically, a man who was trained by Clint in investigative methods.

"This murder had saddened all the police in Panamá, as well as most Panamanians. He will be missed."

"Can you tell us of anything not restricted by the investigation?"

"Yes. Clint left instructions from some time ago that, in the event of his demise, all investigation is to be available to the police and public. He believed strongly in the transparency laws.

"Clint left quite some collection of papers and videos concerning these people, proving they were in a conspiracy to defraud the government and the Ngobe people of their land. One of those videos was of Clint's last moments.

"It does not show the actual shooting. The perpetrator was between Clint and the camera, but it shows more than we need. That is because it is a conspiracy, so it matters not who physically pulled the trigger. Legally, they each and all pulled it.

"We have the original, and have studied it closely. We can know it was not in any way tampered with. If the perpetrators had known of it, they would have destroyed it, not tampered with it.

"Because it cannot be modified, we can show it on television. It does not show the actual murder."

A scene of Clint sitting at the table reading a paper came

on the TV. There was an indistinct sound from a distance. Clint called that he was on the deck. Come on in.

"The cameras are sound and radar directed. They follow the motion, so will move from one to the other," Herrera said.

A man wrapped in towels so only small details could be seen came in and went to move between Clint and the camera.

"Well. So you came back. I've said all I have to say to you," Clint said sharply. "Why the disguise? It could only be one of you three, and the shoes tell me which one."

There was a shot. The form threw the pistol out into the bay and went back to the house and out of sight. Then there was only the picture of Clint slumped over the table.

"The shoes never showed enough for us to identify, but we don't need it. That statement tells us it was definitely one of those conspirators, so they are all equally convicted of murder preplanned."

"What do they say about it? The, uh, conspirators?"

"Exactly what could be expected. That they were together at all times, and that no one went back to Clint's house. As it is a clear conspiracy, as shown by the carefully researched information Clint left, they have no credible alibi. Certainly not with that video!"

"I understand there was another in the conspiracy. A Sr. Penceros?"

"Yes. He was not, according to Clint's investigation, part of it by his own choice. He is and was in Panamá City. As he was unwillingly in the group, had actually helped Clint in his investigation, he will not be charged unless further negative information against him is brought to our attention.

"To the Ngobe Nation and to Clint's family, we wish to

say that the Policía National are in deep grief over this terribly shocking loss to law enforcement, and more because Clint was as much as a personal friend of every honest police officer here and elsewhere."

"We thank you, Capitan Herrera. We in the news also grieve for a lost friend."

"CD, can we talk in private?" Nick Storie said.

"Yes. I think you saw what I saw."

"What's wrong!?" Judi cried.

"Nothing," CD Grimes replied. "This is what Clint worked for. That conspiracy is ended, and will be a lesson to anyone else who tries such a scheme. It's about a piece of evidence the police seem to have missed. It doesn't really affect anything. He's saved the comarca again."

CD and Nick went down to the dock at their place on the island.

"Well, Nick? Was it the hand pushing the surveillance system switch or the rod?"

"Both. Should we point it out to the police?"

"No. It was the only way. I saw the medical report. He had a tumor that would have killed him before he could get the legal stuff together.

"So. He made that recording to that moment and switched it on as he shot himself. I think that rod has a lot to do with it."

"It was in a rod holder, and the tip was pulled back, then the gun was in some kind of setup where it would shoot him, then be flung out into the bay. He rigged that, some-how."

"Note the clip stringer hanging just under where the gun would have to be. I want to know how the gun was held into place and with what? Why wasn't it there?"

"Because it went out with the pistol. It wasn't something that looked like ... those coconut husks! He wedged the pistol into the coconut husk and pointed it where he wanted it. The stringer was tied with a piece of nylon. The nylon had a piece above the knot, just hanging. It was attached to the trigger. Use something to prod the stringer, it pulls the trigger, the recoil yanks a stay off the rod, which snaps into the coconut husk upward. The pistol goes flying out into the bay, the husk drops off the rail, and everything's normal. A rod and reel in a holder and a stringer tied to the rail."

Mathilde, the local psychic/medicine woman, came around in her cayuca and tied to the dock.

"It was the only way. Let it lay." She walked up toward the house.

"I guess we have our orders!" CD said.

Nick nodded.

Tyna handed Mathilde the guanabana chicha and sat.

"Clint communicated with me," Mathilde said. "He wants you to know he is waiting for you. He does not want you to grieve.

"Tyna, he was in great pain, more than most men could tolerate. He had a chance for his death to accomplish something important for us, his people.

"It did.

"He would have died of the tumor in just eleven more days. He would have been unconscious for six of those days. The physical pain would never cease. The pills weren't working.

"He says where he is is almost as much a paradise as this place, that he is in no pain, and will never again be, except the pain of not having you there yet.

"There is no hurry. He can turn time off there.

"He does not stop loving you. Not for a moment. Never. You are and were his happiness, you and the children. He has an amazing capacity for love.

"Nick and CD know he ended it himself in the best way he could that would do the most good for his people.

"Tyna, he is blessed by nature, and is happy. Do not hurt him by grieving. There is no reason to grieve. It has nothing to do with any god. It has to do with the universe and the way things are.

"His love will never die for his people or his family and friends."

"I have never known another man, and I won't. I understand, and won't grieve. I will miss him, every moment.

Terribly."

"No. He says it's alright for you to seek another man. For companionship and sharing. That is a natural thing. He is confident of your love as you were right to be confident of his.

"He says to try out Guillermo. He almost did a time or two, and he's supposed to be the best. You deserve the best."

Tyna laughed. "Now, that is Clint! I can believe you. You are never wrong. You never lie."

"You will live for a long time. Your children and theirs need you. They will always be there for you.

"I must get back to Cusapín."

She stood and went to the dock and to her cayuca. It was a beautiful day. Tyna thought of what Clint said about Guillermo, and smiled to herself.

She would ask Nito about Guillermo. Where Clint would consider it, but not do it, Nito would. Probably had.

"Yo, Clint! What would you say about a mother asking her son if another man was as good in bed as his reputation?" she asked.

She felt Clint's laugh and smile.

C. D. Moulton's works are available on most major outlets as printed or e-books. CD writes the CD Grimes, PI, mysteries, the Det. Lt. Nick Storie mysteries, the Clint Faraday mysteries, the Flight of the Maita science fiction series, books on orchid culture and many others of many types. Mystery, adventure, intrigue, science fiction, humor, fantasy, paranormal, mild erotica, and factual.